Spaceports & Spidersilk

June 2025

Edited by
Marcie Lynn Tentchoff

Spaceports & Spidersilk
June 2025
Edited by Marcie Lynn Tentchoff

All rights reserved. No part of this publication may be reproduced or transmitted in any form or by any means, electronic or mechanical, including photocopying or recording or by any information storage and retrieval systems, without expressed written consent of the author and/or artists.

All characters herein are fictitious, and any resemblance between them and actual people is strictly coincidental.

Story and art copyrights owned by the respective authors and artists
Cover art "Butterfly Fairy" by Vonnie Winslow Crist
Cover design by Marcia A. Borell

First Printing, June 2025

Hiraeth Publishing
P.O. Box 1248
Tularosa, NM 88352
www.hiraethsffh.com
e-mail: hiraethsubs@yahoo.com

Visit www.hiraethsffh.com for science fiction, fantasy, horror, scifaiku, and more. While you are there, visit the Shop for books and more! **Support the small, independent press...**

Stories

12	A Bit O' the Sun by Pamela Love
21	Ideas from the Dry Ocean by Joshua James Jordan
40	Wind Riders of the Perimosphere by CJ Erick
58	The Cursed Coin by Monica Goertzen Hertlein
70	Deep Breath by Aliza Keefer
86	The Best Ice Cream in the Universe by Russell Fee

Poetry

20	The Cackling Clown by Erica Chester
36	How to Watch the Perseid Meteor Shower by Lisa Timpf
37	Grilled Cheese for Sea Monsters by Michael Flowers
55	Eating in Zero Gravity by Eric Taylor
67	Intergalactic Grocery Shopping by Lauren McBride
84	Good Morning! by Jono Mischkot

Illustrations

52	Sea Serpent by Vonnie Winslow Crist
54	Dragonflies by Vonnie Winslow Crist

SALE AT HIRAETH PUBLISHING!!!

BUY ALL THE BOOKS YOU WANT AND USE THIS 20% DISCOUNT CODE: BOOKS2025

GO TO OUR SHOP AT
WWW.HIRAETHSFFH.COM

NO MASKS, NO WAITING, AND WE NEVER CLOSE!

What?

You don't have a subscription to Spaceports & Spidersilk???

(Gasp)

We can fix that!
Just go here and order:

https://www.hiraethsffh.com/product-page/spaceports-and-spidersilk

From the Editor

Greetings, readers, and welcome to the June 2025 issue of Spaceports & Spidersilk.

Today, I, your humble story and poetry collector, want to talk to you about something truly vital, but all too often forgotten in editorials --

Food.

Food is important in so, so many ways. Living creatures require it to survive. Good food can be distracting and enticing, while bad food can make one sick. Feasts often mark celebrations, and families gather together to eat while they talk about their day. Food can be used as a bribe, as a reward, or as the ammunition for a good, messy food fight. Asking a person their favorite food is a classic "get to know you" question.

In many of the tales in this issue, food plays a central part. There are poems herein about the perils of tasting unusual food samples and brewed concoctions, and of the difficulty of eating in an unusual situation. There's even a poem focused on how to properly feed a somewhat odd collection of... pets...?

And then there's the fiction. In this issue's stories we have a simple food portrayed as a wondrous treasure, awful food used as a punishment, and foods used both to attack and lure armies. And, with all that, there's even ice cream for dessert!

That's not to say that food comes up in all of this issue's work, but it does leave me wondering what foods could have appeared in the foodless tales, if the authors had the time and inclination.

But then, that's just food for thought.

Happy eating! I mean, oops, happy reading!

Marcie Lynn Tentchoff

Pyra and the Tektites
Aquarium in Space

Pyra, age thirteen, is running away from home in the Asteroid Belt because she's not doing well in school. Her parents want to send her to Mars for school, and she doesn't want to go. She sneaks aboard a cargo shuttle, and falls asleep in the hold. When she awakens, she finds herself in free-fall; the shuttle has been seized by the Tektites, a group of rebel pirates . . .

. . . and the adventures begin!

Order a copy of the first book of this thrilling adventure series here:

https://www.hiraethsffh.com/product-page/pyra-and-the-tektites-1-by-tyree-campbell

Adopted Child
By Teri Santitoro

Imp, now 13, has awakened from stasis by MA, the ship's computer, to find that everyone else has been killed by a highly infectious disease. She is alone on the ship. But she is about to have visitors.

The *Greentown*, a salvage ship, has spotted a derelict and is about to board her for salvage rights. The crew is blissfully unaware of what happened to the people on the derelict. Soon enough they will find out…but will it be too late? And what of the girl who now controls the derelict?

To everyone involved, everything is new… and potentially lethal.

Ordering Link:

https://www.hiraethsffh.com/product-page/adopted-child-by-t-santitoro

A Bit o' the Sun
Pamela Love

Loading Mrs. Riley's boat wasn't easy this Market Day. The sacks of beans and potatoes to sell were heavy, the eggs were breakable, and her daughter didn't want to get in. "Do I have to, Mother?"

"For the last time, Rosemary, I must be here when Clover's calf is born. You've reached your teens, my girl. There's no reason why you can't take my place at the market for once. Now, into the boat with you."

Step by very slow step, Rosemary obeyed. "But—"

"Whatever's the matter? You can certainly handle the boat." Which was true. Rosemary liked nothing better than taking it out after a hard day's work on their island farm.

"And once you're on the mainland, finding the market's no trouble. Just follow the sound of bargaining!" Mother chuckled.

How can anyone laugh about bargaining? Rosemary wondered. Of course, if she'd spent the last twenty years boasting of her food's quality and arguing over its price every week, she'd feel confident too. For Mother, going to market was almost a game.

But Rosemary rarely saw anyone besides her mother or their few neighbors on the island. She'd only been to the market twice, and hadn't done any selling before. What if she couldn't convince anyone to buy?

She opened her mouth to explain, but Mrs. Riley was already untying the rope holding the boat to the dock. "Just do your best, Rosemary. We won't starve if nobody buys a thing. Now go, or you'll miss the crowd." With a cheerful wave, she headed home.

Gloomily, Rosemary started out. But a light wind, a sunny sky, and a sea smooth as the quilt on her bed soon lifted her spirits. "Mother's right. I may look foolish today, but bargaining's not life or death."

She'd gone almost halfway when it happened. A sudden wave, sharp as a knife, slashed up through the calm sea! It slammed against her boat, rolling it onto one side. For a terrible moment, she thought the boat would flip. Fighting for control, she leaned the other way, gripped one oar with both hands, and shoved it into the water with all her strength. Bit by bit, stroke after powerful stroke, she forced the boat out of danger.

At last she felt safe enough to check for damage. Luckily, she'd lost nothing overboard, and only one egg had fallen from the basket, cracking open on her shoe. Her clothes were wet, but other than that—oh, *no*.

Rosemary didn't want to look down. She could feel what she would see. Little by little, water was creeping over her shoes. This wasn't a small hole to plug; an entire board had come loose. She was in deep trouble. *And soon I'll be in deep water.*

Fitting the board back into place didn't stop the leak. Yanking off her shawl, she tucked it around the gaps, but water still came through. Her heart pounding, Rosemary tried kneeling on the board, which only soaked her skirt.

To buy time, Rosemary heaved the sack of potatoes overboard. But instead of a splash, she heard a soft thump, then a loud roar.

In spite of the danger, she couldn't help but stare, astonished, at the gigantic neck and head that rose before her. Sunlight sparkled on emerald scales. "Glory be!" she whispered. "A sea serpent!"

"How dare you?" he bellowed.

Rosemary was torn between fear and hope. To be sure, the creature was angry—but he was also the only help in sight.

"Sir! Um, serpent?" she began. "I am sorry I dropped my sack on you, but 'twas only to lighten my boat. It's leaking badly."

The sea serpent flexed his neck. "Never mind why, just don't do it again." He plunged beneath the waves.

"Help!" Rosemary shouted. "Serpent, I need your help!"

For a moment she heard nothing but gurgling beneath her boat. She worried as it grew louder, then realized the sound was chuckling.

"You need my help, do you?" the sea serpent asked, surfacing and rolling his eyes. "And why should I bother with the likes of you?"

Rosemary's eyes flashed with anger. "The likes of you" indeed! She knew well enough that he'd caused that disastrous wave. But she forced herself to stay calm. "I'll pay you to carry my boat to the harbor," she said.

"Pay me? I am the wealthiest creature in the sea. Treasure chests overflowing with gold and gems adorn my cave. What treasure do you have?"

Remembering how her mother bargained at the market, Rosemary made herself speak proudly. "I have a sack o' beans, as green as your handsome self. Our farm's never grown finer ones."

"Beans? Bah! Besides, you can't think much of what your farm grows. You've dumped one sack already."

Sea water was now almost to Rosemary's lap. She started scooping as much as possible out with her hands. "Perhaps you would prefer smoked fish? I was planning to eat that myself."

"I have all the fresh fish I want." The sea serpent grinned, showing off his silver teeth. "You have no treasure, then."

Her hopes sinking faster than her boat, Rosemary made herself take a deep breath.

True, she had neither gold nor gems. Then she smiled, because she had something more valuable: an idea. "Have you any pearls?" she asked.

"Thousands," he yawned.

Reaching into her basket, Rosemary took out an egg and held it high. "Like this?"

The monster blinked. "I've never seen an oyster big enough to make that pearl."

"Land oysters are larger," Rosemary fibbed. "A basketful o' these magnificent pearls for a short trip to the mainland harbor —do we have a bargain?"

The sea serpent flexed his coils as he thought it over. "Big they may be, but can they match the quality of sea pearls?" he finally asked.

"Uh..." Rosemary knew that just saying "To be sure!" wouldn't satisfy the monster. He wanted proof. *How can I prove what's not true? If he sees that I've been lying, he could smash this boat like an eggshell—ah-ha!*

The sea serpent was rumbling with impatience when Rosemary laughed. "*Match* their quality? What's in the middle o' a sea oyster's pearl?"

"A grain of sand, or a piece of shell."

Rosemary nodded. "Oysters on the dark sea floor must use such things, for they have nothing better." She cracked an egg against the seat. "Unlike common sea pearls, land pearls are fragile," she explained. Curious, the sea serpent stared at the bright yellow yolk she poured out. "My oysters form pearls around bits o' the sun itself! Now do you see their worth?" asked Rosemary.

The sea serpent boomed, "Agreed. The pearls for safe passage." At his direction, she slid the egg basket's handle over one of his whiskers. Then he dove. Before Rosemary could fear that he was gone for good, she felt a thump beneath her. The sea serpent carried her boat to the harbor balanced on his head, humming as he swam.

Getting the better of a bargain will put anyone in a sunny mood.

New From Hiraeth Publishing!!
Cats and Dogs in Space
By Lisa Timpf

Cats in lab coats, running experiments on *us*. Robot dogs roaming Mars. Space-faring canines who mistake alien vessels for fetch toys. There are just some of the images you'll find in here. With inspiration from myths, news stories, nursery rhymes, personal experience, and a lifelong interest in science fiction, the poems are written in a variety of styles for your reading enjoyment. Reaching from the distant past to the far future, and points in between, *Cats and Dogs in Space* invites you to have some fun re-imagining man's best friend—and whatever it is that cats call themselves.

When we beamed the book to the future, here's what readers had to say:
"Purrfectly delightful! Enjoyable for readers of any stripe. Some of these poems are enough to make a cat laugh!" *Festus, ship's cat aboard the Silver Starr Spaceliner Frederika.*

"Meaty as a prime rib bone, and just as much fun to chew on! I'd give it two thumbs up—if I had opposable thumbs . . . " *Pepper, K-9 Operative, Galactic Space Services*

So there you have it! Get *your* claws on a copy today!

www.hiraethsffh.com/product-page/cats-and-dogs-in-space-by-lisa-timpf

The Cackling Coven
Erica Chester

When witches gather, they make a coven
They keep their cauldron as hot as an oven
They like it boiling to make their brew
Their bubbling, rancid, toxic stew

Their shadows dance around the pot
They throw in innards, ear-wax and snot
This isn't a stew you would like for dinner
Indeed, one spoonful will make you much
    thinner

Two spoonfuls will render you spotty and red
Three spoonfuls and you will simply drop
    dead
So, if you know what's good for you
Stay well away from the witches' brew

In fact, avoid covens altogether
Don't seek them out in any weather
And if thunder's rumbling and lightning's
    crackling
Listen out for a cantankerous cackling

If you hear it, run far far away
Lock yourself in and plan to stay
For witches can be oh so sly
Especially when storms rage across the sky.

Ideas From the Dry Ocean
Joshua James Jordan

The thunder god rumbled in the clouds, and the storm gods went over mountains and land. The god of the underworld pulled out the mooring poles, and the dikes overflowed.
-The Epic of Gilgamesh

Even a killing machine has a soft underbelly. The shark swam overhead with calm, almost unnoticeable strokes of its powerful back fin. A rogue shark, one of the few that migrated before the ocean teemed with them. Sierra admired it rather than the oyster field her opa instructed her to shepherd. She hated it. The starfish never seemed to tire out and stubbornly clung to life. She jabbed them with her whale-bone spear and piled them up, only to come back later to find half of them still alive and slithering away.

She'd rather be the shark than herself. It swam without a care in the world. It didn't need to farm oysters. It went about its business, eating as it may. She liked how the fish swam alongside the shark, but the entire ocean sensed its hunger, darting away and hiding when feeding time came. Nothing was scared of Sierra, even after she jabbed all their stupid friends between the eyes with a bone spear.

Satisfied with her oyster shepherding for one day (besides, Opa would never know she left), Sierra went over to Pavati's fish farm while following closely to the ocean floor, small puffs of sand billowing behind her. She made slow progress since she had to hold her spear in her hand without webbing since that made the most sense. Only some folks had a webless hand or foot. Cato, the boy with the handsome face, said it didn't bother him, which was probably a lie because he kissed Maressa instead, even though she didn't have nearly as lovely hair as Sierra's.

At the fish farm, huge nets the size of whales swayed with the tide just over the ocean floor. Pavati mended one of the nets with a fresh batch of seaweed and a face contorted from frustration.

"Having trouble with that knot?" Sierra asked.

"Yeah." Pavati lifted her hands and backed away from the net. "Can you give it a try?"

"Sure," Sierra dropped her spear and used her webless hand to do most of the tying. "There, all set. Sometimes, it helps to have all your fingers free."

"Doesn't help when you're swimming away from a shark," Pavati said.

"That's what this is for," Sierra said, picking up her spear and thrusting it toward Pavati's face. Pavati pushed it to the side.

Sierra held the spear above her head with both hands and stretched. "Let's go do something fun."

"Like what?" Pavati asked.

"Let's head up and look at the dry ocean."

"That's so boring. It's not even night. The lights aren't even out, and I've got a lot of work to do."

"Sure you do because one fish escaped and swam to the surface. Remember?" Sierra said with a wink.

"Ah, fine. Let's go."

They swam up to the dry ocean and lay on their backs, letting the warm sunlight melt into their skin. They watched the floating white foam in the dry ocean above drift away, apart, and back together again. They did that until a whirring hurt their ears.

"The heck is that?" asked Pavati.

"I don't know. Sounds like a dying pod of dolphins," Sierra said.

A weird thing appeared in the sky, shaped like two bowls stuck together at the rims, spinning with lights all around. It fell into the ocean far off in the distance.

The two friends glanced at each other, one with fear and the other with awe. "No, we're not going to go check it out," Pavati said.

"Oh yes, we are," Sierra said, swimming away. Pavati sighed but followed.

They searched underwater in the direction of the flickering light in the distance. Their flying bowl had disappeared, but they found something much bigger, longer than ten whales, maybe more. The metal exterior was cool to the touch and harder than rock, and then they came upon rows and rows of bubbles.

"There are people in there! People are living in this," Sierra said. A young man in a small room sat at a desk, fiddling around with some tools. Sierra noticed his hands. They were webless. Like hers. "Look, Pavati, do you see? See his hands?" Sierra held up her left hand, comparing it with his.

Pavati grimaced. "Yes, I see." She scanned the ocean above, sensing a shark's hunger. "Alright, we've seen enough now, Sierra. Let's go."

"No way, we just got here. Let's find a way in," Sierra said. So they searched the exterior, passing by letters in a language they knew how to speak but not how to read.

The phrase said in capital letters, "MAXIMUM SECURITY".

***

> *The south wind blew rapidly all day, and the water overwhelmed the people like an attack. The flood frightened the gods, and they retreated to heaven.*

The flood and wind lasted six days and six nights, submerging the land.
-The Epic of Gilgamesh

Sierra and Pavati searched for an entrance, but they only found a hole sucking in water. "If we go in, it would be impossible to swim back out," Pavati said.

"We'll make a rope to climb back out with," Sierra said. They gathered up seaweed and fashioned a rope.

"How long?" Pavati asked.

"As long as we can make it. You can always use it for netting at the farm."

When they finished, they tied the end of the rope to a protruding portion of the sunken vessel, and then Sierra descended into the tube, spear in hand and rope in the other. It grew darker and darker. Louder and louder, like they approached the beating heard of a whale. She reached a bubble lit by red lights like the setting sun. Stepping out of the water, she left the rope on the floor and peeked out of the door, where a long hallway filled with chambers and bars filled the doorways. Someone hummed. Two people yelled at each other, the language familiar but interspersed by foreign words.

Pavati emerged from the water, gasping. Her eyes, wide open and scared, met Sierra's. "This is crazy. Even for you."

"There are people here," Sierra said. "See?" She pointed through the doorway and at the chambers.

Pavati peeked around the corner and then back. "What are they doing?"

Sierra shrugged and almost walked out into the hallway when a loud ring echoed. Metal claws attached to long arms came down from the ceiling, placing a plate into a slot for each room. Slurping, chewing, and grunting ensued.

Sierra's stomach growled. "Maybe we can ask for some."

Pavati rolled her eyes.

Sierra led the way down the hallway with her bone spear stretched out. She felt funny, walking in the air like this. She'd done this maybe once or twice in her life. Pavati crept along behind her.

They approached the first doorway filled with bars. A webless man sat on a cot, devouring food on his plate, when his eyes darted up. He cocked his clean-shaven head, put the plate down, and then ran up to the bars, placing his face between the two of them, his face stretching tight. He had drawings on his skin. One was a demon with blood dripping out of its mouth.

"Sea folk! We got some real sea folk in here," he yelled."Shut up, Frank, you idiot. It's supper," returned another voice.

"No, I'm serious. Come here, let me see you closer," the demon man said.

Sierra shook her head, not sure what to say. She walked further down the hallway. *How many of them were in there?*

Then, the demon man launched between the bars and grabbed Pavati's wrist, pulling her in. He held Pavati's head on both sides. He could snap it in a moment.

"No sudden moves, little missy. Just do as I say, and everything will be okay," he said.

Pavati strained and panicked, her eyes pleading with Sierra to get her out. Sierra lined up her spear between the man's eyes. She'd done this a thousand times. Stabbed through all the starfish in the ocean. He'd be no different. Just bigger and more slimy.

Sierra almost lunged when a rumbling came from the end of the hallway, and a voice yelled," Stop!" She glanced over to see a giant man of metal standing in the hallway. It was like a statue that moved. It had a man's figure but a woman's voice.

"Let her go, Conway, or I'll eject your cell out into the ocean," the statue said with unmoving lips.

The prisoner released Pavati and slouched back into the darkness of his holding room. "I was just playing around."

Turning to face the metal man, Sierra pointed her spear at it in a defensive stance. Pavati got behind her.

"What are you?" Sierra asked.

"A prisoner, like them. Follow my little animatron. I'd like to speak to you face to face." The metal man turned around and walked down the hallway.

Pavati tugged on Sierra's shoulders and pleaded for her to turn back. "It's a witch," she said. Sierra shook her head.

They crept along behind it. It might turn around and smash their heads into the wall at any moment. Down another hallway, up a small flight of stairs, until they reached a modestly sized room with a bunch of windows that somehow showed the outside ocean and most of the rooms they had just passed.

A woman with long, thinning gray hair sat on a chair with wheels. "Hello," the woman said in the same voice as the metal man. "I hope that Gyro didn't startle you. I'm Tesera."

"What is this place?" Sierra asked.

"A place where my people put others that have committed a crime."

"So, you're dangerous?"

"No, no. Some are dangerous with their hands, while others are dangerous with their minds," Tesera said while tapping her head.

"What, like, you can do magic? Like a witch?" Pavati asked. The two girls glanced at each other.

Tesera laughed. "No, more like ideas. Ideas are powerful. As powerful as any magic."

"So, how come you aren't in a room like the rest?" asked Pavati.

"Ideas, remember. I figured out how to escape my cell long ago. Now, this prison, that's the hard part."

"Do you come from somewhere in the Dry Ocean?" Sierra asked.

The older woman grinned, revealing a missing tooth. "Dry Ocean? My, you both are so adorable." She put her hands on the wheels of her chair and rolled back and forth. "Yes, I suppose I am from the dry ocean."

Sierra launched a bevy of other questions until the woman held up her hands and said, "Listen, I'd love to answer all of these. I'll teach you how to answer your questions yourself, but I need you to promise to do something for me first."

"What is it?" Sierra asked.

"Get me out of here."

***

On the seventh day, Gilgamesh released a dove to search for land, which flew away but came back to him. He released a swallow, but it also came back to him. He released a raven which also came back to him. And every manner of bird released. They all came back to him.

So he learned to swim as the fish do.
-The Epic of Gilgamesh

A few days passed, each with instructions on the escape plan and the world in general. Sierra assaulted Tesera with questions, but she always had answers. She even taught Sierra how to use the computers to search for answers using voice commands since Sierra couldn't read. Pavati did not join them, having had her fill of adventure, but she promised to keep quiet about the prison.

"It's like the story of Gilgamesh then. It's kind of true," Sierra said while sitting at the computer.

"What do you mean?" Tesera asked, having never heard the tale. Sierra told her an abridged version. "Yes, I guess somewhat. Except the gods are us. We used comets—" Sierra almost asked, but Tesera knew to explain, "—gigantic balls of ice from the Dry Ocean to flood this world because the people here were our enemies."

"And then the gods made my kind? So that we could survive here?"

"I don't know what made you, but, yes, something designed you and did it well. Maybe the last survivors." Tesera rolled closer to Sierra. "Now, enough history, let's go over the plan again. Today's the day."

Grabbing the model of the supply ship that Tesera had made out of paper mache, Sierra pointed to where she would place the magnet. This would stop the whole ship from working temporarily. Then, she'd make two trips to bring both Tesera and her wheelchair (folded up) onto the ship. After that, slide the magnet off the critical point until the supply ship works again. They had to get it right since the next supply ship wouldn't come for a long, long time.

"Sounds like you've got it," Tesera said. "You're a smart cookie."

"Cookies are sentient in your world?"

Tesera laughed. "Sure."

Sierra got into position in the ocean above the prison, waiting for the supply ship. She got bored and studied the sea, spotting more rogue sharks. The migration school would reach them soon.

The ship finally arrived, and Sierra darted towards the critical point on the vessel's surface. After seeing how quickly it moved through the Dry Ocean, she worried that the ship would move too fast, but in the water, it moved slower than a seastar.

Sierra planted the magnet in the right spot after the ship got close enough to the prison. The vibrations stopped, and the lights dimmed. She swam back to the prison.

"How'd it go?" Tesera asked.

"Perfect."

Tesera slid off the wheelchair and helped Sierra fold it up, which Sierra then carried all the way back to the supply ship.

On her way back to the prison, a black mass loomed in the distance—the sharks.

Sierra darted through the water, pumping her webbed feet so hard that little eddies formed. She burst out and into the chamber where Tesera sat on the floor.

"There's a school of sharks headed this way. They're almost here. We have to wait for the next supply ship."

Tesera's face got red. "No. No. I can't be here anymore. I can't stand it. I'm going crazy here. We're going now. Come on." She slid her way into the water and gasped at its frozen touch. Tesera wore her makeshift breathing mask and waved goodbye to her unresponsive animatron, Gyro. Sierra grabbed her bone spear.

They both swam back up towards the supply ship, but it was so far away that the docking ports were not close to the exit they swam out of. Tesera, swimming with just two arms, was still much slower than Sierra, even while she held the spear.

With one shark, Sierra sensed if it was on the hunt. With thousands of sharks, surely one of them wouldn't mind a snack.

The wave of sharks rolled over, under, and around them. All over. Sierra swam in circles around Tesera, pointing her spear at any shark that got too close. Most veered away at the last second. It almost seemed they would make it to the supply ship without incident.

Then one shark got so close, its jaws wide open, rows and rows of teeth jutting forward, that Sierra stabbed it in the nose. The blood, almost like a dancing crimson fabric, drew an immediate reaction from the surrounding sharks.

They thrashed and bit at everything. Sierra stabbed with her spear until she was nearly exhausted to protect Tesera.

The sharks surrounded them, making it difficult to see where they were going.

After hundreds of jabs with her spear, Sierra grabbed the older woman's hand and seized hold of the shark's fin. "Hold on," Sierra said.

Sierra placed Tesera's two hands onto the shark's side fin and then grabbed the top dorsal fin. She jabbed at its head with her spear, on top to send it down and on the left and right to send it in opposite directions. To send it down, she flipped her body around the shark and jabbed it under its jaw.

Almost there.

The feeding frenzy erupted into a red maelstrom behind them while their living chariot led them closer to the supply ship.

Closer. Almost there.

One shark surged towards Sierra, and she thrust it hard into the nose, the tip of her spear breaking off into its flesh.

Almost.

Letting go of the shark, Sierra moved toward the supply ship. She glanced back to check on Tesera. The older woman slashed at the water with one arm, the other with gash marks and red wisps dancing out of the wounds. She'd lost her breathing mask.

Sierra picked Tesera up under her arms. They got up and into the supply ship, Tesera gasping.

"Are you okay?" Sierra asked.

After swallowing a few lungfuls of air, Tesera said, "Never been more alive."

They patched up Tesera's arm with torn, already-soaked cloth. They set up her wheelchair and waited for the torrent of teeth to move past the ship.

"We did it," Sierra said.

Tesera applied pressure to her arm. "Sure did."

"I'll go out there briefly to slide the magnet off, but I'm coming with you, right?"

"No, sorry. Can't. How would you live where I'm going?" Seeing Sierra's frown, Tesera continued. "But I'll give you this card for access to the prison. Then you can get to the computer and learn anything you want."

"Will I ever see you again?"

"Knowing me, they'll send me right back here in no time."

They hugged, and Sierra went back into the ocean cautiously, swimming out to the top of the supply ship and sliding the magnet over. The lights came back on, and the thrumming of the systems inside began once again. The vessel docked briefly with the prison before returning to the surface. Sierra followed it the whole way, wanting to see it fly through the Dry Ocean. Little waterfalls poured around its edges as it levitated out of the water until it zoomed off almost too fast for Sierra to tell which direction it went.

A few months later, after several learning sessions from the computer, Sierra lay in a bed of seaweed. A fog in her mind wouldn't lift as ideas filled every possible nook, and she had to close her eyes to let them settle. Then, Cato, the handsome boy, and a group of his friends swam over. "Sierra, we're going up to the Dry Ocean. The lights are dancing tonight. Want to come?"

"That? That's a meteor shower. It's dust from space hitting the atmosphere," Sierra said.

She knew she had just used many words they would not understand, and they whispered to each other in hushed tones, one even saying, "She *is* a witch."

"There will be a bigger one next year. I think I will wait for that."

"Have it your way," Cato said, and swam up to the surface, but one boy stayed behind. He was much more plain looking than Cato, but he had big eyes.

"How do you know that?" he asked.

"I know a lot of things," she said.

"Tell me."

"Tell you what?"

"All of it."

He lay next to her on the seaweed and listened to her pour out knowledge unabated. His eyes grew wider with each sentence, and she could see the appreciation for each pearl of insight to the universe. While she had always imagined laying in this seaweed and sharing a kiss with Cato, there was something more wonderful about sharing these ideas instead with him—ideas as powerful as magic.

How to Watch the Perseid Meteor Shower
Lisa Timpf

Choose a clear night
just before mid-August.

Lie back on a tarp or a ground sheet
or lounge in a zero-gravity chair.

If the air feels cool enough,
hunker under a blanket.

Get comfy, but not too comfy;
you don't want to sleep through the show.

Look north, toward Perseus,
intent on streaks of light.

Ignore attention-seeking fireflies.
They're just jealous.

Grilled Cheese for Sea Monsters
Michael Flowers

I live inside a lighthouse,
but it's more a monster bite house.
A lurking in the ocean for a
yummy cheese delight house.
The monsters only like to munch
the soggiest grilled cheese.
I grill them in the evening,
then I rush to fill the seas.
I fling them in the water
with a giant sandwich slingshot,
then light my lighthouse quickly
while the sandwiches are hot.
They see the light and swarm right in
with toothy jaws a-gnashing.
The only thing I see from shore
are fins and tails a-splashing.
Then, all is still—I wonder if
a monster's bit, or hurt.
But, no. They're only still until
I throw cheesecake dessert!

The Adventures of Colo Collins & Tama Toledo in Space and Time
By Tyree Campbell

Out on their first date, high school seniors Colo Collins and Tama Toledo are invited aboard a spaceship and offered the chance to intervene in various events in the Universe. These events can range from stopping an asteroid from striking a planet to helping someone find her house keys. But there's a catch: both Colo and Tama have to agree that an intervention should be performed . . . and sometimes they'll have to perform the intervention themselves!

Ordering Link:

https://www.hiraethsffh.com/product-page/adventures-of-colo-collins-tama-toledo-in-space-and-time-by-tyree-campbell

Wind Riders of the Perimosphere
CJ Erick

Gram was in the closet.

In a shiny lavender jumpsuit, with the words "Flight Patrol" above the chest pocket in black and red lettering.

"Gram?"

"Shhh," she said. "Don't let your mother hear you."

"Why not?"

"Because she thinks I'm a bad influence on you."

Collin's grandmother pushed past him into his bedroom, her metal bracelets jingling. She spied Collin's friend Stacy, who was staring at Gram with a look somewhere between disbelief and disapproval.

"Who's this?" asked Gram.

Collin introduced Stacy, who rose from her cross-legged pillow pose to shake Gram's outstretched hand, jeweled rings and all.

Gram said, "I guess she'll have to come with us." She asked Stacy, "Can you ride an Anaxodon?"

"What's that?" asked Stacy, whose green eyes flowed like lanterns in a nuclear fog.

"Ah, of course you can. Let's go! There's not much time!"

"Wait! We have homework—" Collin tried to say, but Gram grabbed them both by the wrists and dragged them behind her back through the closet, past his cluttered clothes, piles of old games, and the pile of hidden comic books that, at fourteen, his mother thought he should outgrow.

A tunnel that hadn't been there before led from the closet through a maze of rock, bursting out in a vast open-air hangar also made of rock. Inside were at least a hundred people, all in jumpsuits of different colors, white, sky blue, olive drab, yellow and red. A tall blond woman, Commander Frost, saw Gram leading Stacy and Collin across the floor, and strode to intercept them.

"So there you are, Collin," she said. "And about time."

Collin found himself and introduced Stacy. "She'll need to be protected here in the hangar."

Stacy jabbed him with her eyes. "No, I won't. If he can ride an ...ana..."

"Anaxadon," filled in Gram.

"Yes, that," said Stacy, "then so can I."

"I like this girl," said Frost. "Gram Silverspur, please take them to the armorer. We fly in fifteen minutes."

Gram led them toward an oval opening that covered the entire far wall. Great dark silhouettes of nightmare skeletons moved in the light, casting shadows across the floor that they squashed with their running feet.

People ran toward the line of creatures, carrying boxes and cables and woven nets of football-sized globes the color of scorched honey.

"What are those?" asked Stacy.

"Garzhu berries," said Collin. "When they burst, they smell like rotten snakes. Must be big stuff going on."

"It's the Fripernian Frogs," said Gram. "They've broken the treaty and breached the Perimosphere garden wall. If they lay their eggs in Lake Tourmaline, the tadpoles will gobble up all the fish and water fowl chicks and destroy the ecosystem. Thinking about that makes me want to choke a congressman."

"Lake Tourmaline is my favorite place," said Collin. "I mean, after the Beckoncity Library and the Thistletop Mountains."

Gram said, "And no clean water to irrigate the Royal Perimos Fields. People and beasts may starve."

They reached the great hulking shapes, the Anaxodons, dragonflies twenty feet tall and sixty long, facing the open wall ready to launch into the infinite sky beyond. They smelled of tobacco and the underside of a lawn mower, where they cantilevered on six spindly legs in the front and periodically vibrated their long cellophane wings.

One of Commander Frost's flight leaders pointed them to two dragonflies standing side by side with no riders yet. Almost all the other flies were already mounted by a pilot, some not much older than Stacy and him, some well older. They climbed rope ladders to black leather saddles on the Anaxodons' backs, and Gram gave Stacy a quick flying lesson, as if this were some video game and not a real flying creature able to kill and eat them if it wanted. Two pairs of thick hairs stuck out from the backs of the flies' middle segment, two high and two low.

"Pull the low hairs to dive, the high ones to climb. Pull harder on the right side ones to turn right; left for left turn. Got it? Good! Fateful flying!"

She jumped down from the fly's back and sprinted away before they could ask any questions.

Stacy said, "I'm excited as heck, but also scared silly."

"To tell you the truth, so am I," Collin said. "I've only ridden them one time, and that was just to deliver supplies to a stranded convoy."

But Commander Frost soon came to alleive their fears. Calling encouragement up to them where they sat on the bobbing beasts, who seemed anxious to take to the air, where they were most comfortable.

"Go slow at first," said Commander Frost. "Take your time and get the feel. Signal when you're ready by waving the blue flag attached to your saddles."

They gave her thumbs' up, and she strode to the far fly. "Riders! Away!"

One by one the beasts bounded forward and disappeared into the blinding open hangar door. Before he had time to think, it was Collin's turn and he urged the great beast by digging his heels and pulling back on the two upper hairs. As if shot out of a giant's pistol, the fly lurched forward in two great leaps, then the wings buzzed to life behind him and they exploded into bright sunlight...

And below a drop of hundreds of feet to jagged rocks.

Collin jerked his head and eyes back to where they were going, which was straight out into the open sky. He gripped all four control hairs in his hands with steady straight pressure, and glanced back over his shoulder. Stacy's Anaxodon was aloft behind him, curving vaguely to the right. He could see her hunkered down in the saddle, leaning to the left, but the fly continued right.

"Don't lean! Use the hairs!" he called back, over the wind noise and loud buzzing.

She nodded, and her arms moved, and the fly dipped to the left, but soon leveled and pulled up to follow him. Except for a little side to side jitter, she seemed to have learned to control the great beast quickly She always was a quick learner.

They followed the line of Anaxodons for several miles until they began to dive on after another into a wide, verdant green valley, split by a wide blue river. At the far horizon were the lime green and bronze waters of Lake Tourmaline, the bright sunshine glinting off wind-tossed waves. And less than a mile away was a dark line of things moving forward – the Friperian Frogs, seeking to make the lovely lake their own personal breeding grounds.

The flight commander yelled back through a large wooden mega-horn. "Riders – drop your berries just ahead of the frogs, one by one. Follow me."

Collin and Stacy were the last two divers down the line. Ahead, the riders guided their flies into swift power dives like WWII bombers. As they strafed the line, they pulled the amber berries from the nets tied at their hips and tossed them over. By the time Collin and Stacy flew down the line tossing out their bombs, the stink of rotten serpent was strong enough to make him wince.

After he pulled up, Collin looked back to see what damage they had done. Some of the car-sized tan and purple frogs stuck their huge tongues out and turned away, but most leaped over the line of amber berry juice, and continued their hopping and crawling advance on the lake.

"It's not working," he shouted to Stacy.

"What do we do now?" she called back.

"We need help," said Collin. He looked around for more lake dwellers that could help them. Ahead, he spotted a large conical mound of rocks and dirt. Huge red back and red ants moved up and down the hill, leaving empty handed and returning carrying sticks, plants, mushrooms, and wilted flowers.

"There!" he shouted. "We need to recruit the ants. Frogs hate ants, especially giant fire ants! Follow me, riders!"

Collin curved up and away from the lake bank, satisfied to see Stacy and several other riders following him. There was a vast royal vineyard nearby, and he headed straight for it. He guided his Anaxodon down, down to the huge grape wines, which grew in massive trunks on wooden trellises built from tall blue-wood branches. The grapes were nearly ripe, round red spheres larger than the garzhu berries, translucent with foot-sized seeds within. He guided his fly down, and coaxed it to pluck a grape and hand it up to him. He held this grape in his lap, and while the fly pulled another, holding it in its six legs.

"Let's go," he said. "Use them to lead the ants to the frog line."

Collin dropped his first grape near the ant hill, then turned his Anaxodon for another run. The other riders, seven in all, splashed their grapes in red explosions of juice and sugar syrup. The ants paused in their meticulous activity and their antennas twitched in the air. Then almost as one, they moved toward the flat bracelet of red beads on the ground.

The divers splashed their grapes just far enough apart that the ants followed. After the seventh rider dropped her bombs, Collin came in to drop his second. He tapped the Anaxadon's back and it released the grape, and then he saw pink missiles rise from the line of frogs and felt the impacts. He dug in his knees to hang on and pulled back on the hairs. The fly's wings hummed louder, but it stopped as if held on flypaper.

But what held it were four frog tongues, and the owners of those tongues were reeling him in like a flying fish.

Collin dug in his knees again and rattled the hairs. "Go, Naxxie, go!"

The fly lunged against the pull of the frogs, but couldn't break free. They were being pulled to the ground like they were caught in a tractor beam.

From above, Stacy's voice yelled down," What can we do?"

"Find Gram. Tell her we need—"

The dragonfly tilted to the side, nearly throwing Collin off, to his death, since he was still a hundred feet up.

"...tell her we need the herons."

"On it!" she yelled back, and the sound of buzzing wings increased in pitch, but faded in the distance.

Collin twisted back and forth, terrified of the thin pink fleshy cables that attached him to the cavernous dark mouths of the frogs below. What he needed was a light saber or flame thrower or at least his mom's pocket taser. But he didn't have any of those things, and he was helpless to free himself. He and the Anaxodon were now barely seventy feet up and dropping fast. The fly's wings were stuttering; it was getting tired. At any second it might grow exhausted and they would become frog food.

"Sorry, my friend. I should never have gotten us in this close."

At least the ants were having an effect. Streams of the stinging monsters were pouring into the gap between the lake and the frog line, climbing over the slippery suckers and stinging them, sending them bounding back where they had come from. Even if Collin didn't make it, at least Lake Tourmaline and its fabulous biosystem were saved.

Fifty feet now. The Anaxodon lurched harder, buzzed, sputtered, but never gave up. Collin prepared himself for the final plunge.

Then he heard a huge whiffing sound come from across the lake, and huge shadows settled over the land, as if a line of clouds had formed over the lake and was blown by an easterly breeze. And then great tree-trunk like legs dropped from the sky and settled into the shallow water of the lake. The herons had come, like a fantastical natural white canopy held up by yellow ringed stalks. Yellow beaks reached down like godly spear points. A huge yellow and black eye at the top of the closest beak eyed him as it descended.

Gram yelled from somewhere above him. "Cut the tongues!"

Immediately, the closest heron whipped its head to the side and slashed at the four pink cables pulling him down like a pair of scissors. The tongues snapped back and struck the frogs like rubber bands, sending them rolling. Heron beaks lashed out like avian lightning all along the frog line at the remaining hoppers that had not fled the ants. The line fell apart into retreating purple frog backs, bouncing and bounding away into the distance. The herons reared up and spread their wide parachute like wings and squawked so loudly it caused Collin's ears to ring.

"Herons away!" Gram yelled from somewhere above Collin, and the great birds crouched and leaped into the air, flapping away across the lake to their roasting and hunting lands, the shallow swamps and bogs on the west coast. Collin guided his exhausted Anaxodon to a large oak tree and allowed it to rest and breathe in the moist autumn air.

Another fly drifted down to where they lit, and Stacy hovered near him. Her hair was swept back by wind and sweat, and her face was flushed with exertion or excitement or both.

"We did it," she said. "We drove the frogs away."

He nodded, too tired to respond.

***

Gram led Collin and his classmate Stacy back from the Anaxodon hanger, through the rocky tunnel, through Collin's closet and into his bedroom, and said her goodbyes quietly. The clock showed that by modern time, they had only been gone about ten minutes, even though Collin felt like they had fought the giant Friperian Frog invasion for days.

Almost as they settled into their places at Collin's work table, there was a knock at the door, and Collin's mother entered, looking flushed from running the city's housing department from the safety of her office.

"Just checking on you two," Mom said. "You've been very quiet up here. How's the calculus homework going."

"Fine, Mom. Stacy's too smart. She'll blow the curve on the next test for all of us."

Stacy smiled sheepishly, and brushed a lock of sweaty brown hair from her forehead. She realized she was still wearing a rider's glove on one hand, and hid it behind her back.

"No, I won't," Stacy said. "It's really hard."

"So, you've just been studying away up here, eh?" asked Mom, with a raised eyebrow.

"Well, no," said Collin, with a wink. "Actually, Gram came and got us and dragged us through my closet and through a tunnel to Hinterland, where we had to ride giant Anaxodons to drop stinky grazhu berries on marauding giant frogs before they laid eggs in Lake Tourmaline."

Stacy picked up on Collin's ploy.

"But the berries didn't work," she said, "and Colling led me and the other riders to drop grapes in front of the frogs to bring giant fire ants to the rescue."

"But I got trapped by frogs lashing my Anaxodon with their tongues and almost got dragged into their mouths."

"And I found Gram and we brought giant herons to chase the frogs away and cut Collin loose from the tongues."

"Then the frogs hopped away," Collin added. "We had a short celebration, and Gram brought us back here. We're hungry. Can you order us some pizza, Mom?"

Mother's mouth fell open, then she shook her head in mock agitation.

"Video games again, I see. Well, I hope you both do well on your test, or Stacy's parents may not let her come over here to study again."

"No worries, Mom. She's tutored me."

"No, he's helped me."

Mom left the room, shaking her head.

Stacy said, "You've got Anaxodon dust in your hair, dude."

"And you have it on your cheek, girl."

"Fine. When can we do that again?"

"Well, the great lizard march usually happens around Thanksgiving."

"Cool. I'll be a better dragonfly rider than you."

"Ha."

Sea Serpent
Vonnie Winslow Crist

Mellie

The Adventures of a Teenage Vampire

Meet Mellie, an adolescent vampire, as she travels to Italy and New York to discover roots, make friends, and of course get into trouble. Fun adventures for the whole family.

https://www.hiraethsffh.com/product-page/mellie-the-adventures-of-a-teenage-vampire-by-debby-feo

Dragonflies
Vonnie Winslow Crist

Eating in Zero Gravity
Eric Taylor

Of all potential dangers
in exploring outer space,
too little's said of dinner
never staying in its place.

With zero help from gravity,
Peas would float from every plate.
Mashed potatoes drift about,
not having any weight.

Unanchored slops of chocolate sauce —
like comets in the air—
satellite spaghetti
might wind up in your hair.

Tacos, quite impossible—
their fillings floating yonder.
Clouds of soup, and goulash—
Too hazardous to ponder.

Asteroids of applesauce
collide with every chair.
Your glass of milk a milky way:
speckled everywhere.

So would I like to fly to Mars?
Brave ketchup in my ear?
The answer's clearly evident:
I'd rather eat right here.

The Green Lady
By M. R. Williamson

You look at a grandfather's clock—and the clock looks back at you! There's a mist inside it.

You find the words "GET OUT" on the back wall of the closet. In fresh red paint! Still dripping!

A voice from the hay loft screams, "Get out!"

It's the Green Lady of Weeping Willows. What does she want? Well, open the book...

Print:
https://www.hiraethsffh.com/product-page/green-lady-by-m-r-williamson

pdf:
https://www.hiraethsffh.com/product-page/green-lady-by-m-r-williamson-3

ePub:
https://www.hiraethsffh.com/product-page/green-lady-by-m-r-williamson-2

The Cursed Coin
Monica Goertzen Hertlein

Merlynne stared as the carriage rolled to a stop among the farmyard's frost-dead gardens and scrawny chickens. Its golden wheels and ebony sides were too clean, too fine, amidst the litter of broken tools and dirty straw.

The woman inside was tall, with a jewel-studded wig of silver-blonde curls that brushed the top of her velvet-lined carriage. She smelled like roses.

She smiled at Merlynne. "The little girl with magic? Come with me."

She smiled when displaying the room in her castle where Merlynne would sleep, a chamber larger than Merlynne's family's home, with its own hearth. The huge bed had silky sheets and embroidered blankets.

There was even a library where Merlynne was allowed to study and a workroom where she could practice spells and potions.

"I hope you'll be comfortable here, dear."

The Baroness smiled when she invited Merlynne to sit at her table in an enormous room with paintings on the walls and rugs on the floor. The table was so long and full of food, Merlynne expected the entire houseful of servants to join them but it was only her and the Baroness sharing roast venison and white bread and fruits Merlynne did not know the names of.

"Try the mangoes, dear."

The Baroness smiled while showing Merlynne the gardens with secret paths and hidden benches. They smelled of lilacs in spring and roses in summer.

"The pink blooms opened, dear. Have you seen them?"

Later, the smiles only appeared when Merlynne produced an enchantment she requested. "I'm proud of you, dear."

Pleased to receive that special smile of approval, Merlynne shrugged off a growing feeling that the enchantments she was asked to make felt wrong.

Autumn roses in the table centrepiece matched the pink gemstones in the Baroness's tall wig of blonde hair when Merlynne gathered her courage at supper one evening. She told the Baroness how the poisons and curses made her stomach hurt when she cast the spells.

It was the first time the Baroness frowned at her. Merlynne dropped her gaze and fiddled with the lace edging on her sleeves.

"Perhaps you simply need to concentrate harder, dear."

When Merlynne looked up, the Baroness was smiling again. Merlynne nodded.

She kept making enchantments, but she stopped putting her power into them.

***

The Baroness came to the workshop and

watched one day while Merlynne enchanted a coin that would make the bearer ill if he wished harm on the Baroness.

Merlynne fixed her gaze on the coin, fingers clenched on the gold that grew colder as the enchantment was cast until a tinge of frost glittered around its edges. She did not look up, even after the spell was done and the frost melted, even when the Baroness lifted it from her now-lax grip.

The woman held it up to the light slanting through one of the wide windows along the outside wall of the workshop, rolling it between her fingers. Red jewels decorated her wig and her sleeves were tied with red ribbons. Her rose perfume smelled overly sweet, aggravating the upset in Merlynne's gut.

"Is it done to my specifications?"

Merlynne nodded.

The woman's bright blue eyes darted from the coin to Merlynne. "*Exactly* to my specifications?"

Unable to break their gazes, Merlynne swallowed. *A fatal illness*, the Baroness had said. "It...it will be a terrible sickness."

The Baroness did not look away. Her red jewels glittered in her fake hair. "Not a fatal illness, though?"

Despite her quiver of fear, Merlynne shook her head.

The Baroness did not smile. She reached out and took Merlynne's hand, opened her limp fingers, and pressed the coin into her palm. It was warm from the Baroness's grip.

"I want the person to die. It's a fitting punishment for wishing me harm, don't you agree?"

Merlynne's hand shook, encased between the Baroness's warm fingers. "No."

For a long moment, the Baroness stared into her eyes. Merlynne's heart pounded in her chest. The hand in the Baroness's grip grew so warm the coin was slippery with sweat.

Then suddenly, the Baroness released her. She looked thoughtfully around the workshop. "I think we can find a more suitable place for you to work. Perhaps somewhere that allows you to concentrate better, don't you think?"

She smiled, but it made Merlynne's insides shiver.

The new workshop had no windows. It was at the bottom of a long flight of narrow stone stairs. It was chilly and the walls were mildewed.

She set the gold coin on a workbench in a corner. The next day, she put a book on top of it.

She continued to make the charms for bountiful crops and healthy animals but she stopped making enchantments to catch thieves or curse poachers.

No invitations came to join the Baroness at supper. Rye bread and brackish water were delivered to her room morning and night. One of the servants, a man with thick arms and no neck, followed Merlynne from her bedchamber to the workroom and back, barring her way if she headed for the gardens.

She did not see the Baroness for a fortnight, nor any of the servants except the one without a neck, but some mornings she found that items in the workshop had been moved: a book open to a different page, a cauldron lifted and put back not quite in the same place.

***

One afternoon, as Merlynne completed a talisman to make pigs fat, the workshop door opened. She froze as the Baroness walked in, looking around before going straight to the book on the corner workbench. She lifted it and picked up the gold piece.

She tilted her head and looked at Merlynne. Diamonds in her tall wig sparkled like ice chips. "Is the coin finished?"

"I...I don't know what you mean." Bile burned the back of Merlynne's throat. Her hands balled at her sides, but she held the Baroness's gaze.

The blonde woman set the coin down and left the workshop without smiling. When Merlynne could move again, she edged close enough to slide the book back over the coin.

That evening when Merlynne tried the workshop door, it was latched from outside.

She shouted, but no one answered. She waited, but no one delivered food.

She flipped through the books, looking for a spell that would unlock a door, but her practise attempts only made the latch rattle. She stopped practising when she heard bootsteps on the stone staircase. She held her breath rather than shout for help.

The next day, she huddled on the dirt floor, shivering, and tried to banish thoughts of the Baroness's long table full of meat and gravy and warm bread and stewed plums. She wondered if the garden had become brittle stalks.

Would she damn her own soul if she prayed for the Baroness to die?

In the morning, Merlynne heard the workshop door open and close. On the floor was a loaf of stale rye bread and a hunk of mouldy cheese along with a pitcher of water. Merlynne ate it all as fast as she could and then sat, praying her rolling stomach would hold it in.

When the Baroness arrived, Merlynne still sat on the floor of the workshop beside the empty pitcher, trying not to vomit. She looked up through bleary eyes. From the floor, the emeralds in the Baroness's tall wig seemed impossibly high above.

A hint of the old smile crossed the Baroness's thin lips. Then she went directly to the table in the corner, picked up the coin, tossed it in the air, and caught it. She set it back down and walked out without a word.

Merlynne stopped staring at the door and sat staring at the coin.

***

The big man gripped Merlynne's shoulder tightly. The bruises would be dark and deep.

Despite the pain, Merlynne was glad. The only reason to have her dragged from her basement cell to this wing, a wing that had been off-limits even when Merlynne was still in her mistress's favour, was that the Baroness was angry. Furious. Defeated.

The servant's meaty fist knocked gently on a set of double-wide, carved wooden doors inlaid with gold.

Then it swung inwards, pulled by a sour-faced maid barely older than Merlynne.

In the centre of the room, on a wide bed draped with gauzy white linen hangings edged in lace and embroidered bedclothes scented with lavender, the Baroness lay.

In spite of the lavender, the room smelled of vomit and antiseptic.

Perhaps it was the enormous bed, or the absence of her tall wig, but the Baroness looked small. Even frail.

Her real hair was wispy and soaked with sweat, stuck to her forehead. Her cheeks were sunken and her skin pallid.

But her eyes were sharp and full of hate. Even knowing the woman was too ill to physically strike, Merlynne stepped back.

The big man shoved her, sending her

stumbling towards the bed. She caught herself and stood, hands folded, waiting for the Baroness to speak. Waiting to begin negotiation.

The sour-faced maid dipped a silk cloth in a pan of water and touched it to her mistress's brow. She winced when the Baroness slapped her hand away.

The Baroness never took her malevolent gaze from Merlynne. "Is this curse fatal?"

"Yes, milady." *As instructed.*

"You can be executed for this." The Baroness coughed, setting off a fit of wheezing and gasping.

"Yes, milady. If you die." Merlynne nearly wished for that. Was the woman spiteful enough to die so that Merlynne would be burned at the stake?

For a moment, the hatred in those sharp eyes flared brighter. Then the Baroness lay back on her mound of lace-edged pillows to catch her breath.

Her gaze narrowed but the blazing anger was replaced by ice-cold calculation. "What is your price?"

Though anxiety pierced down her spine, Merlynne looked the Baroness in the eye. "Safe passage."

In the ensuing silence, broken only by the Baroness's wheezing breaths, Merlynne forced herself to remain still, chin high, gaze locked with her adversary.

Finally, the Baroness nodded. "Done. But

if you return, if I even hear word of you from anyone in this barony, our deal is void."

Heart pounding, mind spinning with the need to remain calm until she left this woman's presence, Merlynne nodded in return.

Another fit of coughing wracked the Baroness before she lay back. "Do it."

Merlynne stepped forward and held out a hand. "Give me the coin."

The Baroness gestured at the big man standing behind Merlynne. He pulled the gold coin from a pocket and placed it in Merlynne's palm.

Once she had hold of the source, she cast the spells that would drive out the black magic. As it broke, she had an impression of thick black ooze running out and sinking through the floor, dispersing into the earth. When it was done, she dropped the coin on the floor and wiped her hand on her skirt as if soiled.

The Baroness drew a deep breath without any rattling wheeze. She pinned Merlynne with a glare. "Now go."

Spinning, Merlynne bolted from the room. She raced out the garden door, through the rows of wilted roses, and across frost-tipped fields.

Finally, her legs aching, her breath short, she knelt in the dirt and bowed her head. She prayed for her family, for her safe journey, for the servants at the barony, even the man with no neck, and for the Baroness herself.

    Then she got to her feet, shook out her skirt, and began walking.

originally published in The Lorelei Signal October, 2023

Intergalactic Grocery Shopping
Lauren McBride

Don't
taste the
aliens'
fresh-food samples!
And
if
something moves - walk
by quickly
with eyes
down.

Aliens, Magic, and Monsters
By Lauren McBride

Fun to read. Fun to write. *Aliens, Magic, and Monsters* features poems set in the unlimited and imaginative realm of science fiction, fantasy, and horror. The poems were chosen to showcase over twenty poetic forms from acrostiku to zip, from strict rhyme to free verse, and much more in between. There are guidelines included on how to write each type of poem. Try a sci(na)ku. At only six words, it's sure to interest even the youngest readers.

Type: Juvenile and Young Adult Poetry Manual
Ordering links:
Print: https://www.hiraethsffh.com/product-page/aliens-magic-and-monsters-by-lauren-mcbride

ePub: https://www.hiraethsffh.com/product-page/aliens-magic-and-monsters-by-lauren-mcbride-2

PDF: https://www.hiraethsffh.com/product-page/aliens-magic-and-monsters-by-lauren-mcbride-1

Aliza Keefer is a middle school student from Arizona, who is enrolled in her school's Writing for Publication elective course. She has been published in Scribere and was awarded second place in a poetry contest at her local library. In her free time, Aliza enjoys playing basketball, drawing nature, and reading works of Rick Riordan.

Deep Breath
Aliza Keefer

Boom! Cannonfire and gumption. That was Cassandra's life. Aliens and space warlords, starfood and danger. But also laughter and adventures and the most beautiful view of the stars.

Cassandra Deepsea sailed through the galaxy on her ship, "The Pearl of the Sky" with her crewmates, as she had for five years. She loved to breathe in the crisp air from her golden oxygen mask. Every day offered some unexpected danger, some strange new experience, some exciting revelation; and she loved it.

She stood at the stern of her craft facing to the front. Then she twirled around, leapt to the central mast, clasped the rigging with her bejeweled fingers, and started to climb. Cassandra reached the crow's nest and hoisted herself into it as her crew scurried about on the deck.

She straightened her loose captain's shirt and took a deep breath. Then Cassandra pulled out her telescope and popped it into shape. When she looked into it, she saw a small gray sphere in the distance. The gravity bubble around the ship warped the planet into a spherical oval.

"All hands on deck!" she shouted as she collapsed her telescope and slid it into her bloomers. "Planet ho!"

Everyone on deck quickened their pace, battening the hatches, tying in the rigging, and securing the belowdecks. Cassandra laughed and shimmied down the mast. The sound rang in the air as she strode over to the helm, where she took the wheel in her hands and spun it. She flipped her brown hair, displaying the natural highlights that streaked it.

"Cass! That's Pluto! It's dangerous!" Rusty, the ginger quartermaster, called to her.

"Of course! That's what I live for!" Cassandra laughed and twirled around the quarterdeck. Her mates shifted uneasily.

"Er, don' you think we had 'nuff time horsin' 'round? I wanna go home" one said. Voices of assent echoed throughout the crew.

Cassandra's smile vanished. "What do you mean, Scaley?" She held out her hands and twirled around. "We are home."

"We have beds and food, not a home. I have a family on Jupiter." he responded.

"Aye!" the crew chorused.

"Well..." Cassandra hesitated. The crew fell silent looking at her carefully. "We're pirates, we live for danger and excitement. I certainly do. I'm sure you can wait a few more months."

The crew glared at her but cautiously went back to their work. Rusty came up to her and wrung his hands. "Cassie, I don' think the crew is very happy with yeh." he said nervously as she steered the ship. "Yeh don' want a mutiny, do yeh?"

"A mutiny!? Please! They wouldn't dare!" she scoffed. "Besides, I've already set the course for Pluto. We'll be there within days."

Rusty looked scared but returned to his kitchen. Cassandra stepped up to the balcony and took a deep breath. Pluto had clouds shrouding its form. She felt her spirits lift as the ship steadily moved forward. The stars that twinkled in the distance winked at her and danced merrily.

Despite the noxious gas, grubby barbarians, and giant earthworms that inhabited Pluto, Cassandra felt excited for their arrival. Cassandra's parents were originally two of the barbarians, but when she was born, they moved to Jupiter, a more hospitable planet. Yet Cassandra couldn't wait to see her home planet. One fateful day, five years ago, a crew of pirates captured her. However, their captain, Captain Wisecrack, took pity on her miserable, eleven year old self and took her under his wing. Ever since then, Cassandra felt a calling toward Pluto, and when Wisecrack died two years ago, leaving the captaincy to her, the calling had only intensified.

She got a gleam in her eye and ran down the steps to the bow where she planted a foot on the bowsprit. She stepped up and spread her arms in order to keep her balance. Then she whooped and ran along the narrow beam to the edge where she stood on her toes and leaned forward.

Suddenly Cassandra felt a small push from behind and teetered on the edge of the pole waving her arms frantically. She fell into space and felt fear bloom in her chest. The gravity bubble pulled her down slowly until she was almost touching the gravity boundary. She twisted around and flailed her arms. She clasped the end of the bowsprit and pulled herself up. She crawled along the plank until she stood on the deck again.

"Who did it!" she shouted. "WHO PUSHED ME!"

Cassandra stomped up to the quarterdeck and clapped her hands. The crew froze and looked at her. Adrenaline caused her heart to beat quickly and her brain to be on high alert. She glared at them all. She clapped once more and the crew clambered into a line. Then they placed their hands behind their backs.

"Scaley Ironclaw, Rusty, Tommy Crab, Bill Carver, Salty Stone, and One-leg Bobby," Cassandra strode along the line and said the names as she passed the man. "Scabby Knife, Hooky, Sharky, Minnowtail, Kevin

Knuckle, and Will. Which one of you did it?" she spoke slowly and dangerously.

"I did, Captain." Cassandra turned toward the voice, drew her cutlass, and pressed it up against Sharky's throat.

"What!" she said.

"I had som't'n ter tell yeh. But yeh were runnin' 'long the 'sprit." Sharky said, his eyes bulging. "I went up ter talk t' yeh but I lost me balance, yeh see. I ax'dent'ly pushed yeh but I were scared yeh thought it were on purpose, so I ran 'way."

Cassandra took the blade from his throat and stared him in the eyes. "You're lucky I'm not feeling threatened, otherwise you'd be walking the plank without an oxygen mask." she said dangerously. "Move along!"

The crew resumed their work and cast glances at Cassandra warily. Her chest heaved and she stomped over to the captain's cabin. She opened the door, walked in and slammed the door shut. She collapsed onto her bed shaking with adrenaline. The memory of almost being lost in space flashed in her mind, and she started sobbing.

She knew that the crew was always opposed to making someone so young captain, but she had thought that she had proven herself to them. She quickly forced her tears down. Maybe they wanted a dangerous captain, one who only cared about themself. She leaned back into her bed and curled into a ball, resolving to try to be the captain they wanted her to be.

***

Cassandra awoke to silence. She sat up in her bed and stretched. Starlight trickled in through the small porthole and danced on the floor. She yawned and lugged herself out of bed. She was halfway through pulling her jacket on when she froze. Everything was eerily silent.

She yanked on her boots and slammed open the door. All the hands above deck froze and stood to attention. Cassandra narrowed her eyes and strode about the deck searching for anything amiss.

"As you were," she said. The mates resumed their silent work of trimming the rigging and battening the hatches. Cassandra loped up to the quarterdeck and grasped the helm wheel. She squinted into the distance and saw Pluto. Something looked different about it. She cocked her head, searching for an angle that would reveal the cause.

"G'mornin', Cap'n Cassandra! How'd yeh sleep?" Cassandra jumped as Scaley addressed her. "I told the men ter be quiet so yeh can sleep. I knew yeh was shook up a bit from yesterday."

"I can sleep just fine without silence," she told him, hoping she wasn't being too harsh. "When I woke up, I thought something was amiss."

"Oh don't worry yerself 'bout that, I've got it covered." Scaley grinned.

Cassandra glared at him but turned back to her view of Pluto. The planet looked blurred somehow as if covered by a fog or viewed from a great distance. Somehow, Pluto looked farther away than it had been in the night.

Was that just a trick of the starlight? Was the warp of the gravity bubble affecting her view? Or had someone steered the ship away from Pluto, away from her destiny and away from her home?

Confusion bubbled up in Cassandra's chest and she reminded herself to be stern and harsh. "Which one of you scalleywags steered *The Pearl* further away from Pluto in the night?" she asked, trying to be dangerously calm.

The men looked at her and then at Pluto and finally around at themselves. Confusion was clear on their faces.

"Er, cap'n? Pluto don' look farther 'way." One-leg Bobby proffered. "Are yeh sure she moved backwards while yeh slept?"

Cassandra narrowed her eyes and bared her cutlass. "Are you doubting my word or challenging it?" she asked him, forcing confidence.

His face paled and he fidgeted with his belt. "Neither cap'n. I mean' no disrespect"

She returned her blade to its sheath. "Right. Then, who changed the course?"

Rusty stepped forward and removed his cap. "Permission ter speak?" Cassandra nodded. "I- I know these lads an' they're as loyal as dogs, they are." Somebody coughed. "If *The Pearl* did go backwards in the night, I- I don' think it any fault of them or I."

Rusty backed into the crowd and returned his hat to his head. Cassandra's face remained impassive, but she gestured for them to go back to their work. The sound and scuffle of the rigging and the helm replaced the silence and filled the air.

"Scaley!" Cassandra called, imperiously then bit her lip. The former saluted. "My quarters, now!" She strode into her cabin and awaited her first mate. The eyes of the crew followed Scaley as he followed after her and shut the door.

"Wots goin' on?" Scaley asked.

Cassandra braced her hands on her desk and leaned forward. She closed her eyes and took a deep breath. Worry bloomed on Scaley's face as he took a step forward. She sensed the movement and looked up.

"I don't know, Scaley. That's the problem. I don't know." She sighed and pinched the bridge of her oxygen mask. She closed her eyes, hung her head, and let out a small sob. Concern masked Scaley's face as she straightened and wiped away her tears.

Suddenly, she lunged toward him and seized his shirt. "Please, Scaley, you're close with the boys. Please! Are they trying to kill me? Are they mutinying? Am I a bad captain?"

Scaley pushed her away and led her to her chair. "Oh, Cass! Rusty told yeh, those men ar loyal as dogs. An' that's exac'ly why.." He drew his sword and pressed it against her throat. "I needed to take charge. They may be loyal to yeh bu' they're so tired o' the same ol' thing." His eyes were steeled and sad. "Yer too young ter be cap'n. An' yer won't ev'n list'n ter yer crew!"

Fear shone in Cassandra's eyes as the blade cut into her neck. "Why?" she asked, her chest heaving with a sob. "I tried to be a good leader, I- you were my family."

Scaley leaned in so his mouth practically touched her ear. "Tha's jus' it, yeh were ignorant!" His hot breath sent shivers of fear down her body. "We never had any say, and we never got to the things we wanted to do. Always on the move, we were. I'm tired, we all are. Ne'er any break for us. You don' deserve our loyalty."

Cassandra gasped. "I can change! You can rest. Everything can go back to normal!"

"No," Scaley looked sadly at her. "We've been under you long enough."

He reached down and removed her cutlass from her belt. Scaley cast it aside, reached into his bloomers, and pulled out a spool of rope. Pain sliced her nerves as he tied the rope cruelly tight around her wrists.

"Get up!" he snarled as he pulled his cutlass back..

Cassandra stood unsteadily and staggered forward. She tripped and fell forward, but before she hit the deck he grasped her bindings and hauled her up painfully. She gasped aloud from the pain. Scaley gently steadied her and pushed her from behind toward the door. Once she stood before the door, he reached around her and pushed it open.

The crew paused in their work when the door opened. A few looked surprised to see her bound. Cassandra stood up straight and tall but her hands desperately struggled behind her back. Scaley prodded her forward. As she walked, a few of her men sneered and laughed. Her eyes watered in shame. Even the stars themselves seemed to be laughing at her.

Suddenly a ceramic glass smacked her side and fell to the floor, where it shattered. She looked up to see who threw it, but they all smirked now. She felt a bruise forming where the chalice had hit her ribs. A few of the men opened the hatch and beckoned her forward. She was about to step down when she wondered if Rusty was involved. She turned back and scanned the crowd but saw no sign of him. She must have been standing for too long, because the men pushed her roughly down the stairs.

The berth held the hammocks for the men, the guns, and the infirmary. Cassandra hoped they would lead her to the hammocks, but they led her down the second flight of stairs to the cargo hold. Her guards pulled her across the hold and chained her to the wall. She resisted their rough hands pushing her toward the wall and struggled to remain upright as they knocked her down, but it was no use. They chained her feet to a lead ball but left her hands in their rope bonds. Then they returned to the deck.

Cassandra huddled against the wall. Before she could stop herself, she felt hot tears running down her face. How could her crew do this to her? What had she done wrong? As soon as the questions bloomed in her head, she shut them down.

Of course. This was a test, her chance to prove herself to the crew. All she had to do was escape and prove she was ready. She felt along the inside of her boot for the small knife she kept hidden there and pulled it out. She awkwardly turned it backward and started to cut the rope on her wrists. After a few minutes of work the rope fell away. Cassandra took a deep breath and rubbed her wrists. Now all she needed was a plan.

***

Cassandra awoke to the shuffling of large bodies. She opened her eyes and squinted in the bright starlight streaming from the porthole. With the realization that the guards were coming in, she seized her rope and convincingly wrapped it around her wrists.

The door opened. Scaley entered and was followed by the two guards. Scaley surveyed her for a second before stepping forward and hoisting her up. She stumbled but caught herself before she fell. The guards snickered.

"Come on!" Scaley said, kneeling down to unlock her feet. The lock clicked and he straightened. He then unsheathed his cutlass and prodded her forward. She willingly exited the cargo hold and walked straight up past the berth to the main deck

The entire crew huddled around the hatch. They looked up expectantly as the door opened. A few of the men smiled cruelly as they saw her bound. Others looked resigned. The rest looked sadly away.

Cassandra searched the crowd for Rusty. He stood to the side near the back of the pirates. He refused to meet her eyes. Hurt and devastation swirled inside her heart as anger formed in her mind.

However, Cassandra refused to be broken. She straightened and forced dignity to reclaim her face. She strode forward ahead of the blade at her back and did her best to scrounge up the confidence to meet the eyes of her crew.

The men formed a line on either side of her. Her eyes followed their rank and saw at the end was the plank. She felt oddly confident as she walked along the ranks despite the jeers and cruel jokes made at her expense. The expanse of space before her mocked her with its beauty and frightened her with its unknown. Scaley kept his sword at her back until they reached the base of the plank, where he swung her around to face the men.

"Before yeh is the tyrant, yeh were forced ter work under. Bu' now, we're in charge an' nobody gon' stop us." he declared. The crew cheered and shouted. Scaley reached behind to unclasp her oxygen mask. Before he could, Cassandra let go of the rope around her wrist, knocked Scaley's hand away from her head, seized his cutlass, and placed it against his neck. The crew jumped up and drew their swords.

"There! I proved myself. Can we go back to the way things were before now?" Cassandra asked. The crew looked confused. Suddenly Scaley laughed and the rest of the crew followed suit.

"Yeh think this is a test?" he chuckled. "Well i's not. We gave you chance aft'r chance. Yet you chose ter be ar'gant ev'n when we tried ter guide yeh. Yeh don' deserve ter cap'n."

Cassandra gasped and stepped back, releasing Scaley. All that time she was being horrible to her crew, and she thought she was helping them. Her vision turned blurry. How could she have been so cruel.

Suddenly, pain flared on her shoulder. Kevin Knuckle had cut her with his knife.

"That's for keep'n me 'way from me fam'ly" he said. The others stepped up and each in turn sliced with their knife.

"You blamed me." Sharky said.

"Aye and did'n listen" Will cried. They all shouted in agreement as Cassandra gaped at them bleeding from many wounds.

Finally Rusty stepped up looking resigned but hurt. "Yeh treated me like scum." he choked.

"Aye!" the whole crew shouted

Scaley stepped up. "Yeh treated all o' us like scum." He reached for the strap of her oxygen mask.

Cassandra pleaded with her eyes. "Scaley, please I know I did you wrong. We can steer away from Pluto and I- I can be a lowly deckhand. I- I thought I was doing what you wanted me to do; to be all self righteous and such. Please, I know I don't deserve your forgiveness but-"

"You thought we wanted a heartless leader?" Scaly cut her off. He hesitated but wrenched off her oxygen mask. "Well, think again."

He pushed her back against the railing and she fell backward into the gravity bubble. She held her breath, reaching around and clasping the railing to look at her crew. They stared at her with hard eyes. Then she steeled herself, resigning herself to her fate and let go, falling to the bottom of the gravity bubble and sinking through.

Dark space enveloped her with its grasp. Euphoria filled her. Tears streamed down her face but her mind was panicked. The darkness was black and endless. She had the sudden realization that she would never find out what was awaiting her. Her legacy and her destiny would never come to pass. She would never be able to see her parents again, or hug her little sister, or… or..

But that was all so insignificant. She deserved her fate as harsh as it was. She lost sight of *The Pearl*, and the cheers of the men faded out of range. Pain bloomed in her lungs, and she closed her eyes. Painful minutes that passed felt like eternities.

Then the pain started to dim and Cassandra's mind felt at ease. The stars twinkled brightly and the planets smiled at her. And one of them was Pluto.

The darkness seemed welcoming and inviting. She remembered the pain of the hold and the deck and wished the darkness would just envelope her forever. Her cuts had healed, and her lungs felt no strain.

Bright light filled her vision, and she let go of the breath she had been holding. The light consumed her mind and brought with it an absolute peace. Cassandra felt a soft smile on her lips as she closed her eyes, relaxed her muscles, and felt the life leave her body.

Good Morning!
Jono Mischkot

When the sun sets beneath the sea,
The slugs wake from waterlogged dreams,
As squids sip seaweed tea,
And octopi stretch their tangled feet.

While we on earth fitfully sleep,
The ocean ripples with energy.
Hammerheads carefully brushing their teeth;
Troops of seahorses patrolling in threes.

And electric eels recharge their tails,
As sea turtles reluctantly slip on their shells.
And orcas fin-bump humpback whales,
And dolphins diligently deliver the mail.

And the sun warms the colder crowds,
As boneless jellies quiver like clouds,
And the ocean floor's adorned in a shroud
Of silver-scaled mackerel and rainbow trout.

And the sun falls further still,
Illuminating anglers and translucent krill,
As blobfish warble like rolling hills,
And stingrays chatter like movie reels.

Life unfolding minute by minute;
Aquatic cries, laughing limpets;
A chorus of coral humming resplendent;
Tidal tunes that burble transcendent.

But eventually the sun must rise,
Returning to its proper place in the sky,
As we yawn and fret and stretch and sigh,

The Best Ice Cream in the Universe
Russell Fee

My uncle Gerry Karlsson was a storyteller – a great one. My cousins and I loved his stories and even loved the fact that they changed a bit – sometimes a lot – with each retelling. We'd all listen closely for any new twists, colorful additions, or shifting exaggerations; and thrilled at pointing them out to him. But one of his stories never changed no matter how many times he told it, not by a single word. It was the one he said was true. The one that he swore actually happened – to him.

Gerry was the youngest child in a family of proud Wisconsin dairy farmers. But his family's real passion was ice cream. They made ice cream on the farm and sold it in a small shop in town. Before he was in high school, Gerry had become the best ice cream maker in the family. The family's recipes for a dozen assorted flavors became so popular with the townspeople and with all the farm families in the county that after a year in business, his father put a sign above the store that announced: *Karlsson's Ice Cream, The Best in the World*. No one argued with that claim.

One day a new customer came into the store and ordered butter pecan. After only a few licks of the two scoops atop his waffle cone, the customer declared that Karlsson's ice cream was not only the best in the world but was the best in the whole universe. The next day, Gerry's father put up a new sign. This one proclaimed: *Karlsson's Ice Cream, The Best in the Universe.* After that, the family couldn't sell its ice cream fast enough. The boost in sales kept their dairy cows very busy, and new t-shirts with *Karlsson's Ice Cream, The Best in the Universe* printed on the front generated even more sales. Gerry and his family wore them when working at the store and most other times as well to advertise the business.

One night Gerry and his older brother closed shop and headed home in the family car. The night was unusually dark. Low rolling clouds extinguished any light from the stars and moon. The road was visible only as far as the car's weak headlights could stretch before the night swallowed them. Tall fields of corn hemmed the road, hiding any beacon of light from the few farmhouses along the way. The rumble of the car drowned out all sounds except for the piercing crackle of the crickets and the coarse rustle of corn stalks in the car's wake.

The dark and hush made Gerry a little afraid. He was beginning to imagine a host of scary scenes when he heard a loud pop. The car shuddered, swerved onto the road's gravel shoulder, and stopped. Gerry and his brother got out of the car and inspected it. One of the rear tires was flat, the rubber shredded. And they didn't have a spare. Their dad would have to come with the tractor to get them and pull the car home. Gerry's brother assigned him the task of walking to the nearest farmhouse to use the phone to call their father. He would stay with the car until Gerry returned.

Gerry began the walk to the nearby Foley farm. Mr. and Mrs. Foley were both ancient, no longer farmed, and lived by themselves in a worn-out, clapboard house next to an empty, sagging barn. Gerry hoped they would be awake when he got there. As he walked, the sounds of the night surrounded him. There were howls of coyotes, the mournful hoots of owls, the unseen but felt darts of bats above him, and the rush of invisible beings through the cornfield. The crunch and dry rattle from the corn stalks grew louder and closer. The darkness magnified the sounds, and Gerry imagined frightening things stalking him with malice in their hearts. The night grew even darker, and he wasn't sure anymore where the Foley farmhouse was.

He started to run back to the car but stopped when the clouds parted and the moonlight revealed the dirt path that led to the Foley house. As he stepped onto the path, a shooting star streaked overhead followed by a bright flash behind the old home. The dirt path was rutted and uneven and Gerry stumbled and tripped several times in the dark before he finally reached the house. He climbed the porch stairs, dusted himself off, and knocked on the door. But no one came. He knocked again, louder this time, but the door remained closed. He called out to Mr. and Mrs. Foley but got no answer. He knocked once more, harder this time. The door opened a crack, but no one peeked out. Gerry pushed the door, and it slowly swung into an empty living room. Before he entered, he loudly announced his presence, but again no one answered. Gerry then stepped into the house. A light shimmered through the partially opened door to the kitchen.

Gerry crept toward the kitchen and peered through the crack in the doorway. His eyes fell on a blood-curdling scene. He froze in fear, unable to move a muscle. Mr. and Mrs. Foley lay on the kitchen table, their bodies stiff and unmoving like toppled marble statues, their eyes wide in terror, their mouths open in a silent scream. Around the table, hunched over them, squirmed six tall, thin, beings with long arms, bulbous heads, and giant bulging eyes. Their bodies radiated with a greenish glow, their hands clenched and unclenched with long needle-like fingers, and glinting knife-like teeth shown from their gaping mouths.

Suddenly a dozen giant eyes blazed toward him. In his head, he heard these words in a low scratchy growl, "You have interrupted our meal. We have traveled far and are hungry. You look tasty. We will eat you next." Gerry tried to run but couldn't. His limbs were like stone. He tried to scream for help, but no sound came.

One of the beings floated toward Gerry and its needled hands reached to grab him. But just before they dug into his flesh, he heard a voice in his head say, "Stop."

One of the beings joined the other in front of Gerry and glowered at him. Then, with its sharp fingers, it plucked at Gerry's t-shirt and lowered its face to examine it. "Is it true"' asked the voice.

Although Gerry couldn't speak, in his mind he asked, "Is what true?"

The voice responded with, "Is it true Karlsson's ice cream is the best in the universe?"

"Everyone says so," said Gerry in his mind.

All the beings bobbed and spun. Their razor-edged teeth vanished and were replaced with what looked like smiles to Gerry. Then the voice said, "We have traveled to ten thousand galaxies searching for the treasure of ice cream. It is the greatest delicacy and most delicious food in all the universe. The beings in every world crave it. We must have it."

"I know the recipe. If I give it to you, will you spare us and leave?" said Gerry in his mind.

The voices in Gerry's head chanted, "Yes, yes."

And then, because he was his father's son, he had an idea. "And will you keep my family's name on the ice cream for all time?" he added.

"Yes, yes, yes," chimed the voices"

And so, Gerry gave away the family's secret ice cream recipes to the space aliens.

Gerry watched from the back porch with Mr. and Mrs. Foley as creatures' spaceship rose from the ground, hovered in the air for an instant, and then shot up into the night sky, disappearing into a tiny white dot among the stars. As he headed back to the car and his waiting brother, Gerry wondered if someday, far into the future, travelers from earth to another planet would find a sign that said, *Karlsson's Ice Cream, The Best in the Universe.*"

Stop euthanizing healthy dogs!!

Go to the Animal Rescue Shelters and give a dog a home!